SNOW

ISAO SASAKI

THE VIKING PRESS, NEW YORK

First American Edition
Copyright © Kodansha Ltd., Tokyo, 1980
All rights reserved
Published in 1982 by The Viking Press
625 Madison Avenue, New York, N.Y. 10022
Published simultaneously in Canada by
Penguin Books Canada Limited
Printed in Japan by Kyodo Printing Ltd.
1 2 3 4 5 86 85 84 83 82

Library of Congress Cataloging in Publication Data
Sasaki, Isao.   Snow.
Summary: Trains come and go at a small train station on a snowy day.
[1. Railroads—Stations—Fiction. 2. Snow—Fiction.
3. Stories without words] I. Title.
PZ7.S24865Sn   [E]   82-2659   ISBN 0-670-65364-0   AACR2

E
SAS

Sasaki, Isao

Snow

DATE			
8 '83	SEP 30 '85	APR 14	FEB 23
NOV 23 '83	OCT 14 '85	MAY 12 '86	OCT 15
DEC 22 '83	OCT 28	MAY 26	FEB 22
AB(H,m)	DEC 2 '85	SEP 24	FEB 13
OCT 31 '84	DEC 18 '85	OCT 8 '86	MAR 9
Nov. 16 '84	JAN 6 '86	DEC 8 '86	MAR 6
JAN 28 '85			NOV 27
FEB 28 JIV MAR 18 '85		DEC 10 '86	DEC 13
MAR 19 '85	JAN 13 '86	JAN 23 '87	
MAR '85	JAN 20 '86	14	MAR
MAY 13 '86	JAN 27 '86	JAN 31	MAR
OCT 14 '85	FEB 17 '86	JAN 30	MAY 31
			OCT 13

© THE BAKER & TAYLOR CO.